Date: 10/17/16

J GRA 741.5 BEN
Coudray, Philippe.
Benjamin Bear in Bright Ideas! : a
Toon book /

PALM BEACH COUNTY
LIBRARY SYSTEM
3650 SUMMIT BLVD.
WEST PALM BEACH, FL 33406

# BENJAMIN
# BEAR

*in*

BRIGHT IDEAS!

## PHILIPPE COUDRAY

# BENJAMIN BEAR

IN

## BRIGHT IDEAS!

A TOON BOOK BY

# PHILIPPE COUDRAY

# For my godson, Nicolas

Editorial Director: FRANÇOISE MOULY  ·  Book Design: FRANÇOISE MOULY & JONATHAN BENNETT

Translation: LEIGH STEIN  ·  PHILIPPE COUDRAY's artwork was drawn in india ink and colored digitally.

**ABDOPUBLISHING.COM**

Reinforced library bound edition published in 2016 by Spotlight, a division of ABDO
PO Box 398166, Minneapolis, Minnesota 55439. Spotlight produces high-quality reinforced library bound
editions for schools and libraries. Published by agreement with TOON Books.

Printed in the United States of America, North Mankato, Minnesota.
092015
012016

THIS BOOK CONTAINS
RECYCLED MATERIALS

A
TOON
BOOK

w w w . **TOON - BOOKS** . c o m

A TOON Book™ © 2013 Philippe Coudray & TOON Books, an imprint of RAW Junior, LLC, 27 Greene Street,
New York, NY 10013. No part of this book may be used or reproduced in any manner whatsoever without written
permission except in the case of brief quotations embodied in critical articles and reviews. TOON Books®,
LITTLE LIT® and TOON Into Reading™ are trademarks of RAW Junior, LLC. All rights reserved.

## LIBRARY OF CONGRESS CATALOGING-IN-PUBLICATION DATA

*This book was previously cataloged with the following information:*

Coudray, Philippe.
 Benjamin Bear in "Bright ideas!" : a TOON book / by Philippe Coudray.
 p. cm.
Summary: Benjamin Bear, accompanied by his faithful rabbit friend, continues to share his observations and
questions about the world around him.
ISBN 978-1-935179-22-1
1.  Graphic novels. [1. Graphic novels. 2. Bears--Fiction. 3. Humorous stories.] I. Title. II. Title: Bright ideas!
PZ7.7.C68Bd 2013
741.5'973--dc23

          2012022895

ISBN 978-1-61479-423-3 (reinforced library bound edition)

**Spotlight**

A Division of ABDO
abdopublishing.com

## *Treetop*

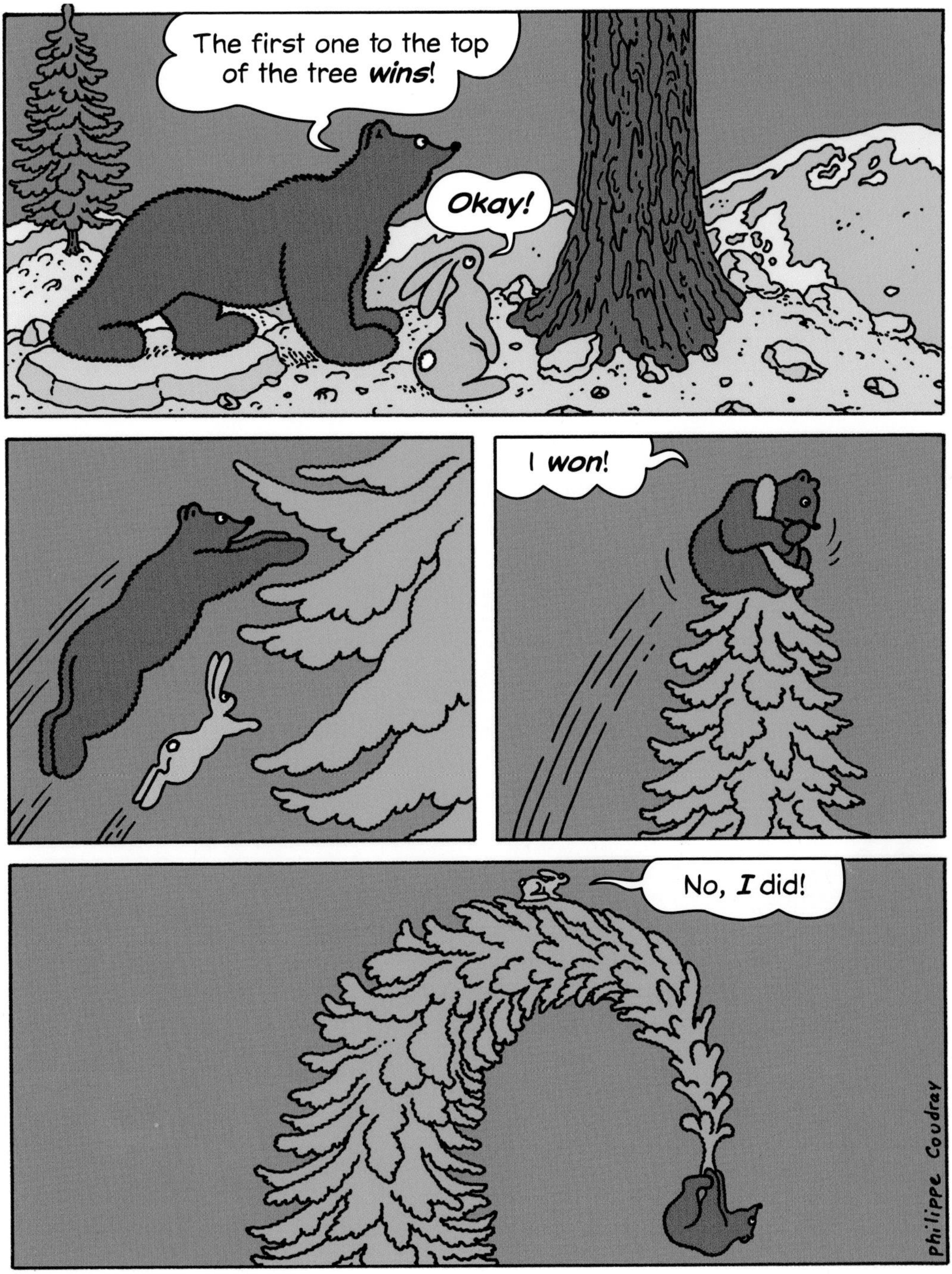
The first one to the top of the tree *wins*!
*Okay!*
I *won*!
No, *I* did!
philippe Coudray

## *Good catch*

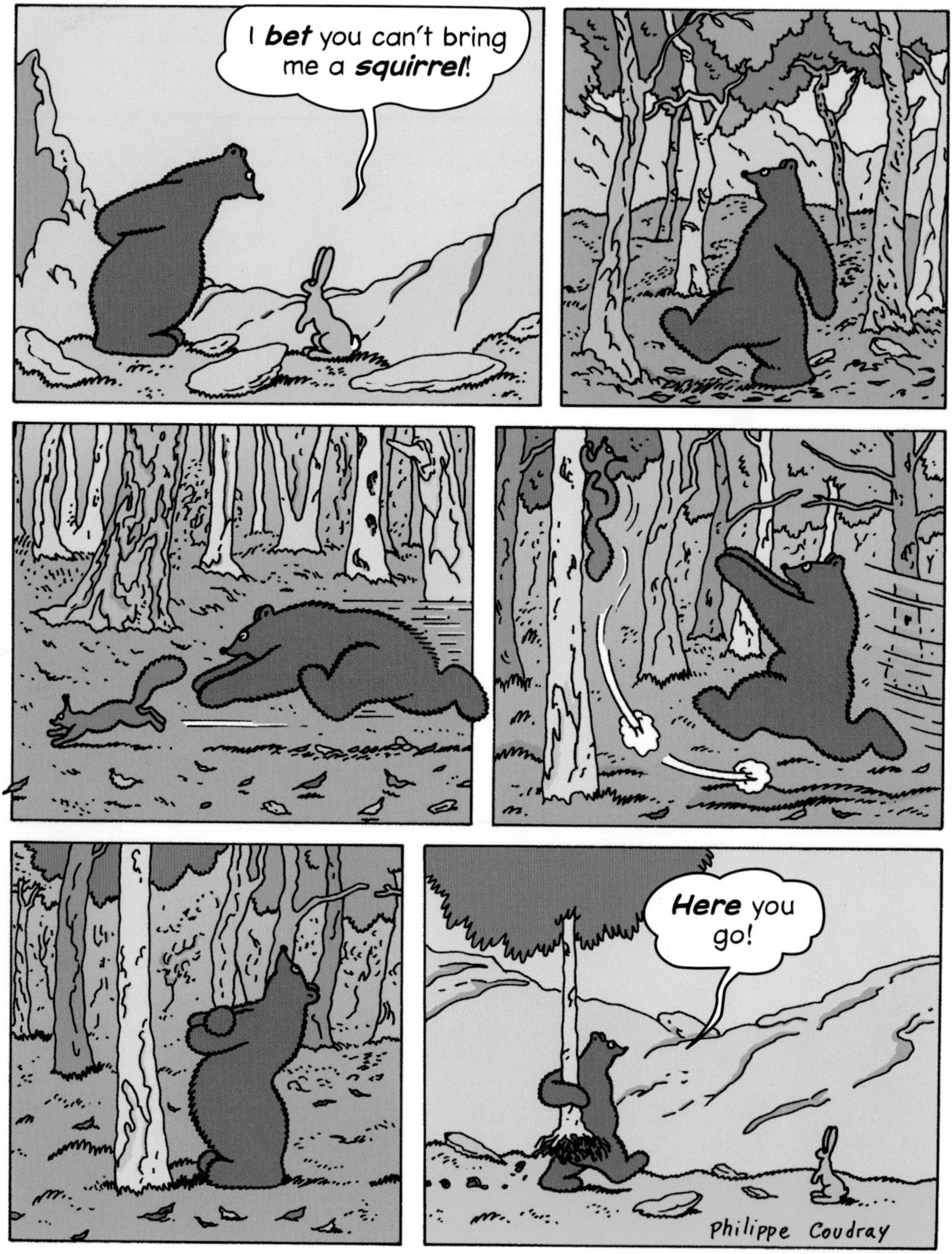
I **bet** you can't bring me a **squirrel**!
**Here** you go!
Philippe Coudray

## *Sharing*

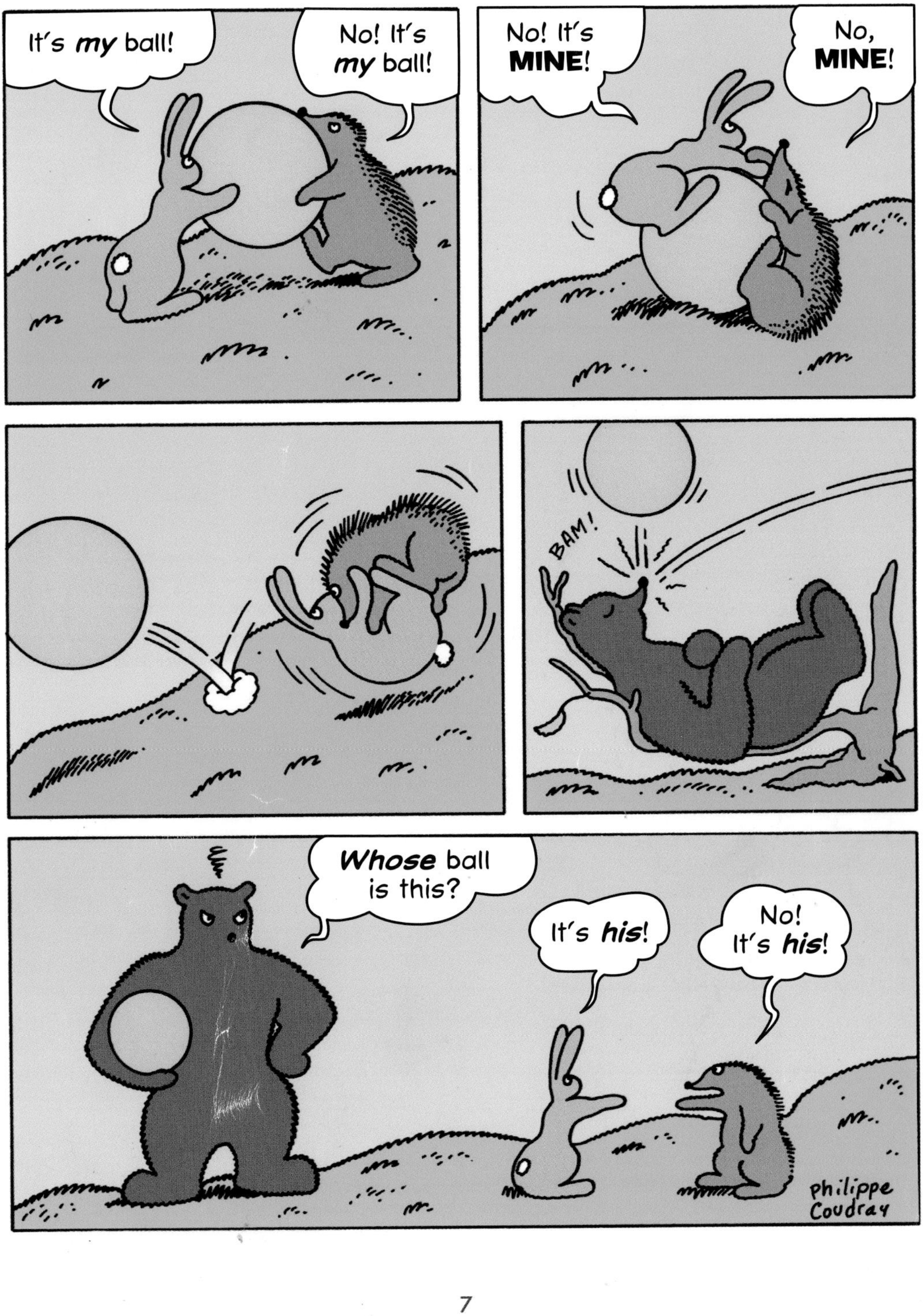
It's *my* ball!
No! It's *my* ball!
No! It's **MINE**!
No, **MINE**!
BAM!
*Whose* ball is this?
It's *his*!
No! It's *his*!
Philippe Coudray

**See-saw**

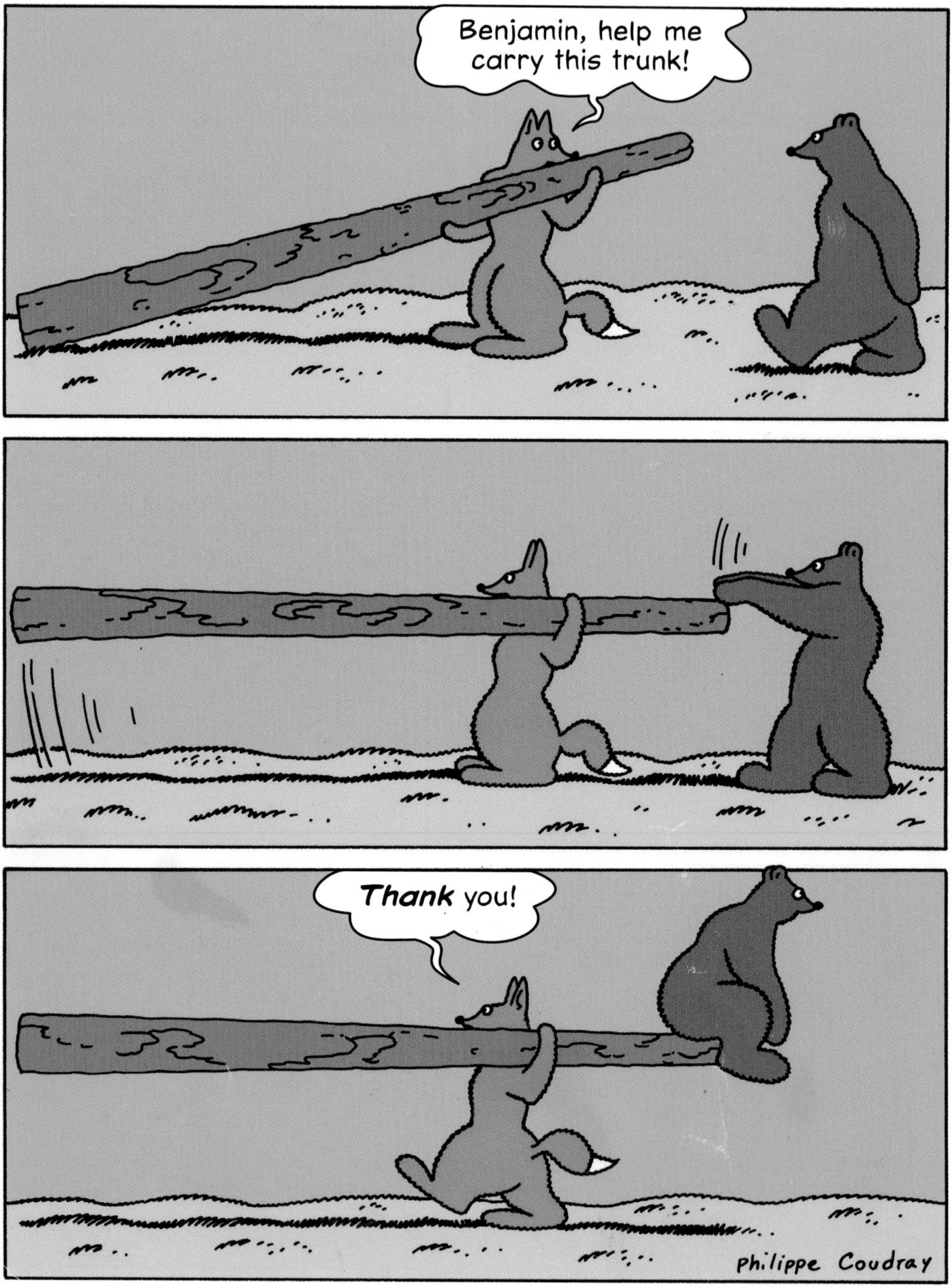
Benjamin, help me carry this trunk!
Thank you!
Philippe Coudray

## Crossing

Philippe Coudray

9

## Can I get a ride?

Philippe Coudray

## The ladder

Philippe Coudray

11

## *High wire*

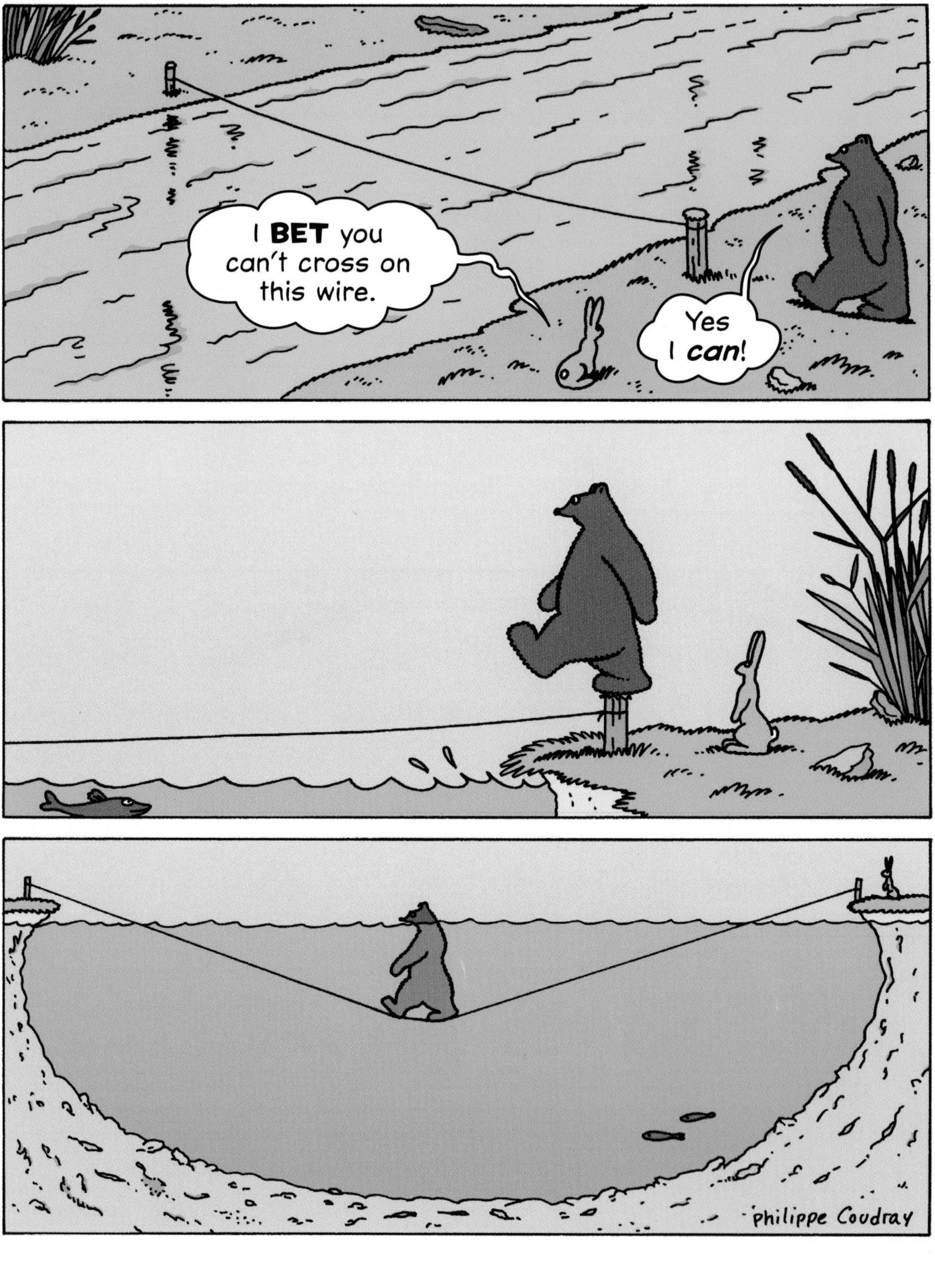
I **BET** you can't cross on this wire.
Yes I *can*!
philippe Coudray

## *Like a fish to water*

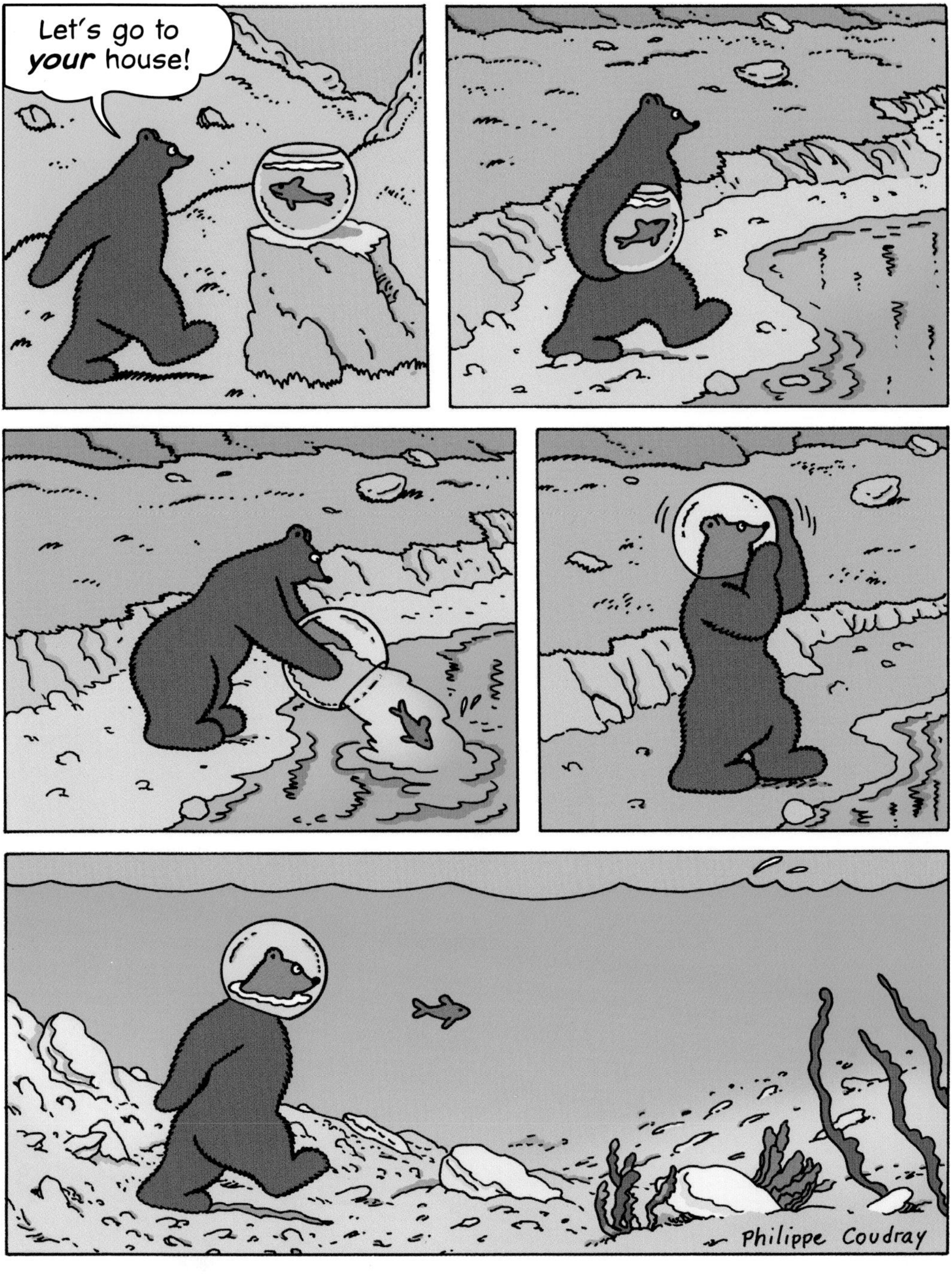
Let's go to *your* house!
Philippe Coudray

## Keep going

Philippe Coudray

14

## Follow the leader

Philippe Coudray

15

## *Hot and cold*

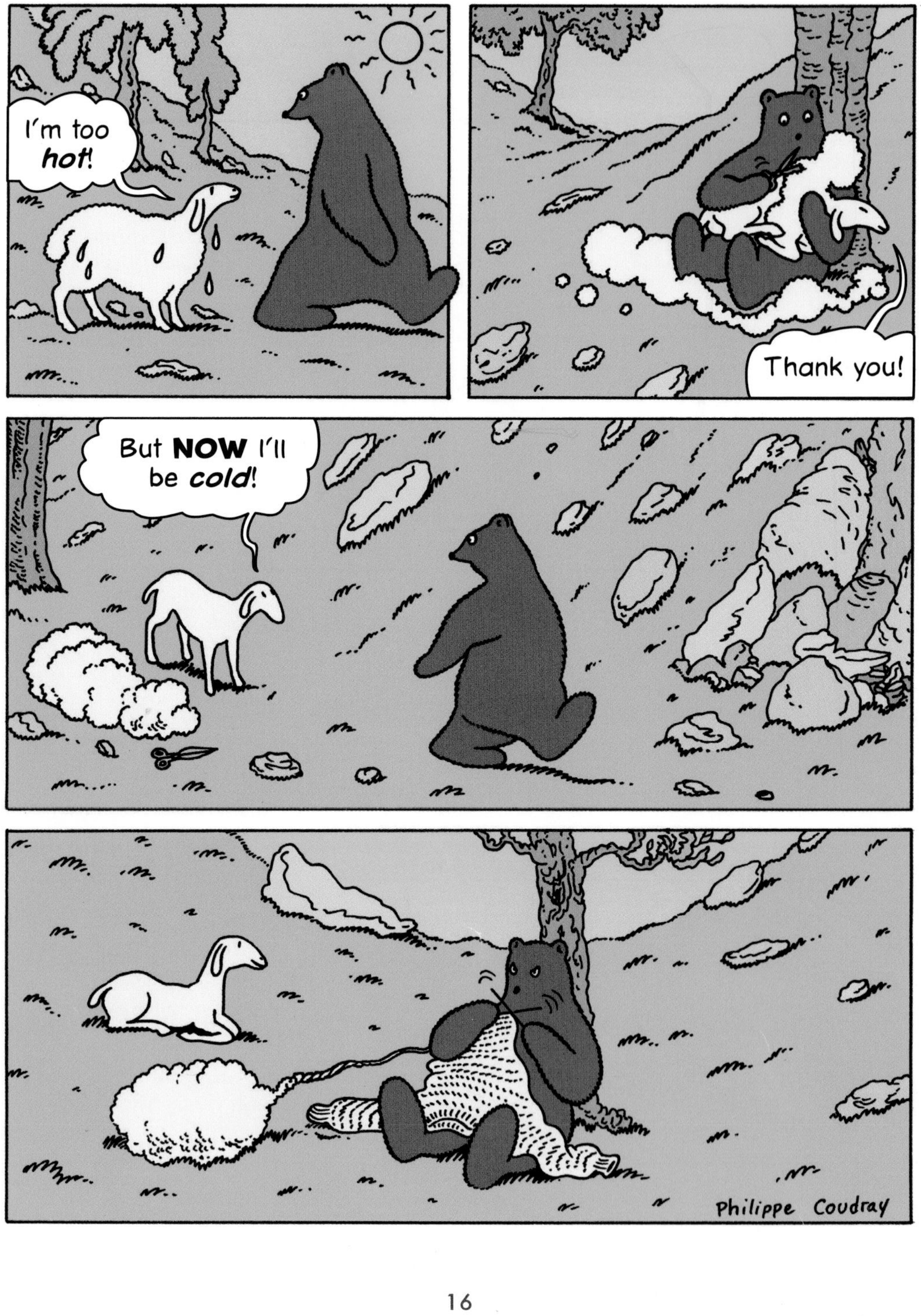
I'm too *hot*!
Thank you!
But **NOW** I'll be *cold*!
Philippe Coudray

## Spring cleaning

philippe Coudray

## *Stay close*

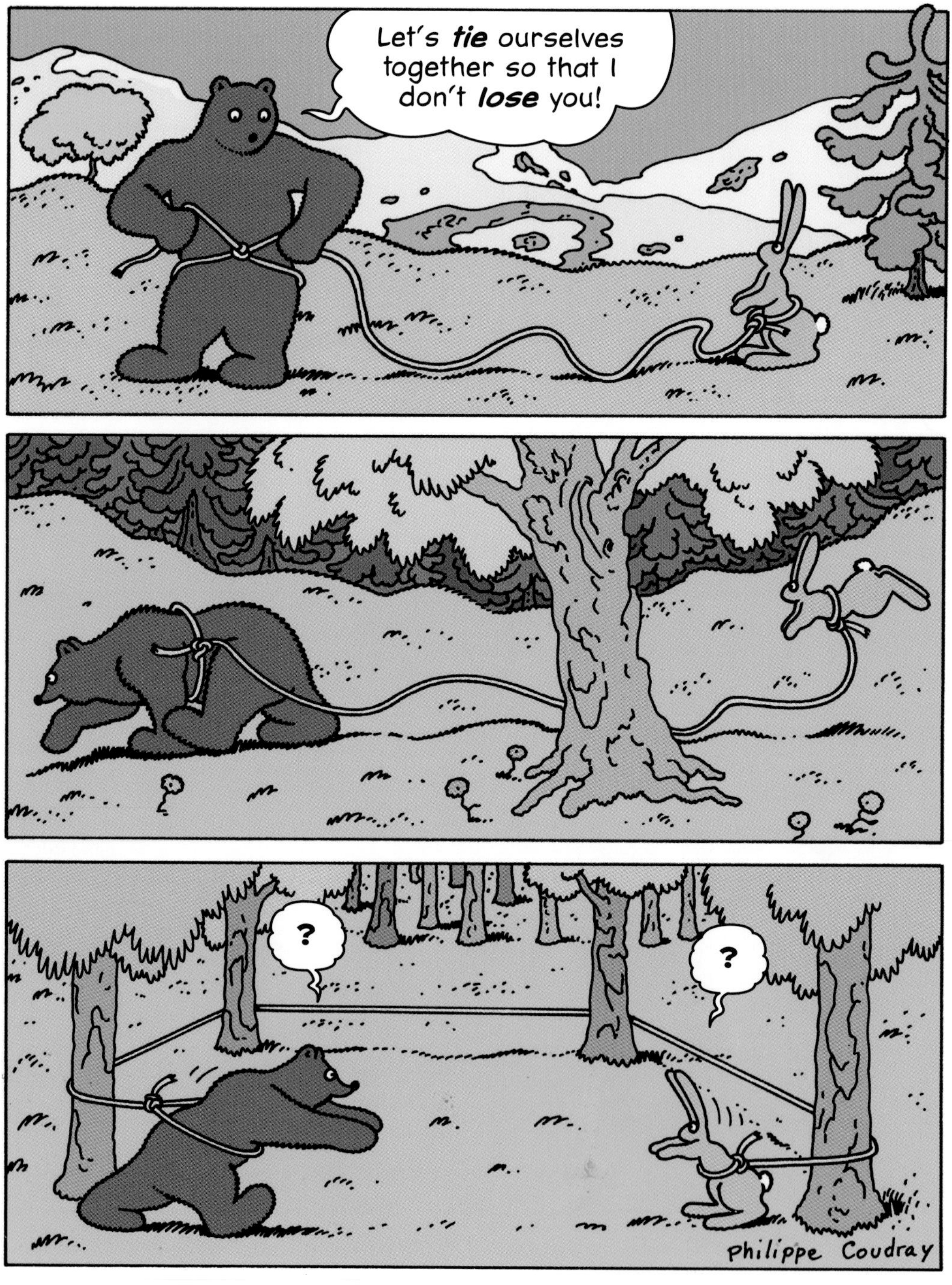
Let's *tie* ourselves together so that I don't *lose* you!
?
?
Philippe Coudray

## Something out of nothing

Philippe Coudray

**It's raining...**

Philippe Coudray

## Portrait

Philippe Coudray

## *A good night's sleep*

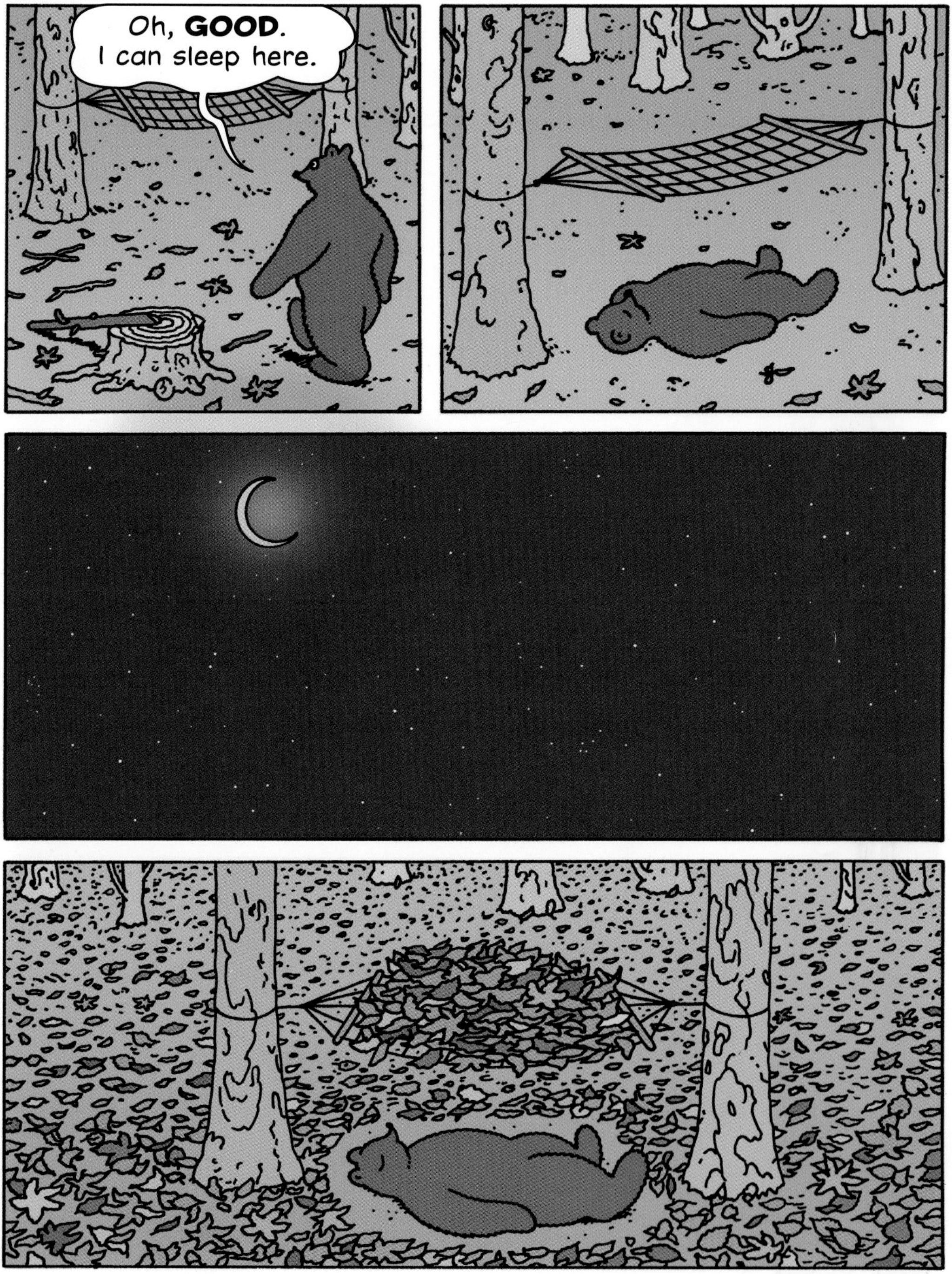

Oh, **GOOD**.
I can sleep here.

## Two for one

Philippe Coudray

23

## The house

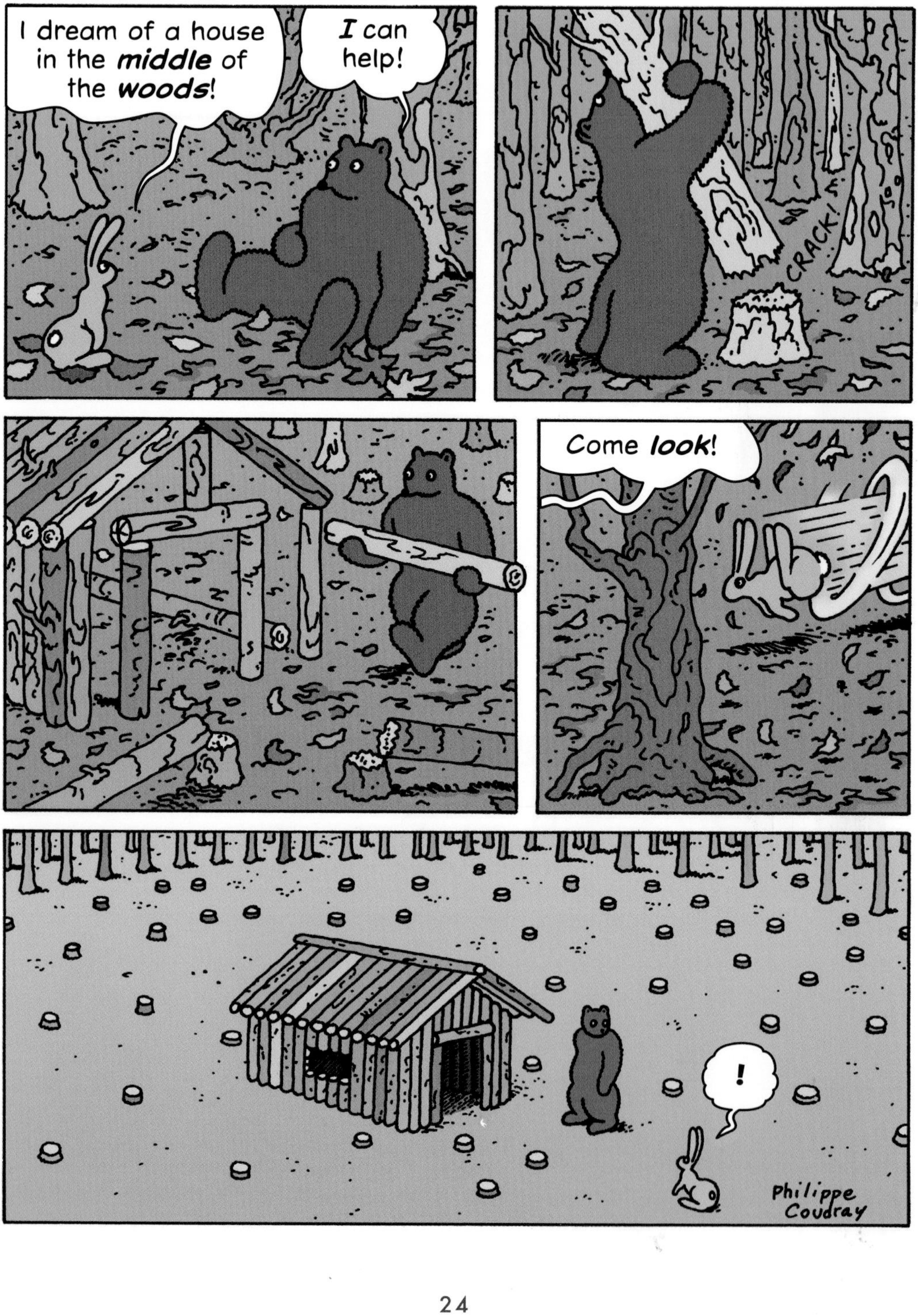

I dream of a house in the *middle* of the *woods*!
*I* can help!
CRACK!
Come *look*!
!
Philippe Coudray

## *Air mail*

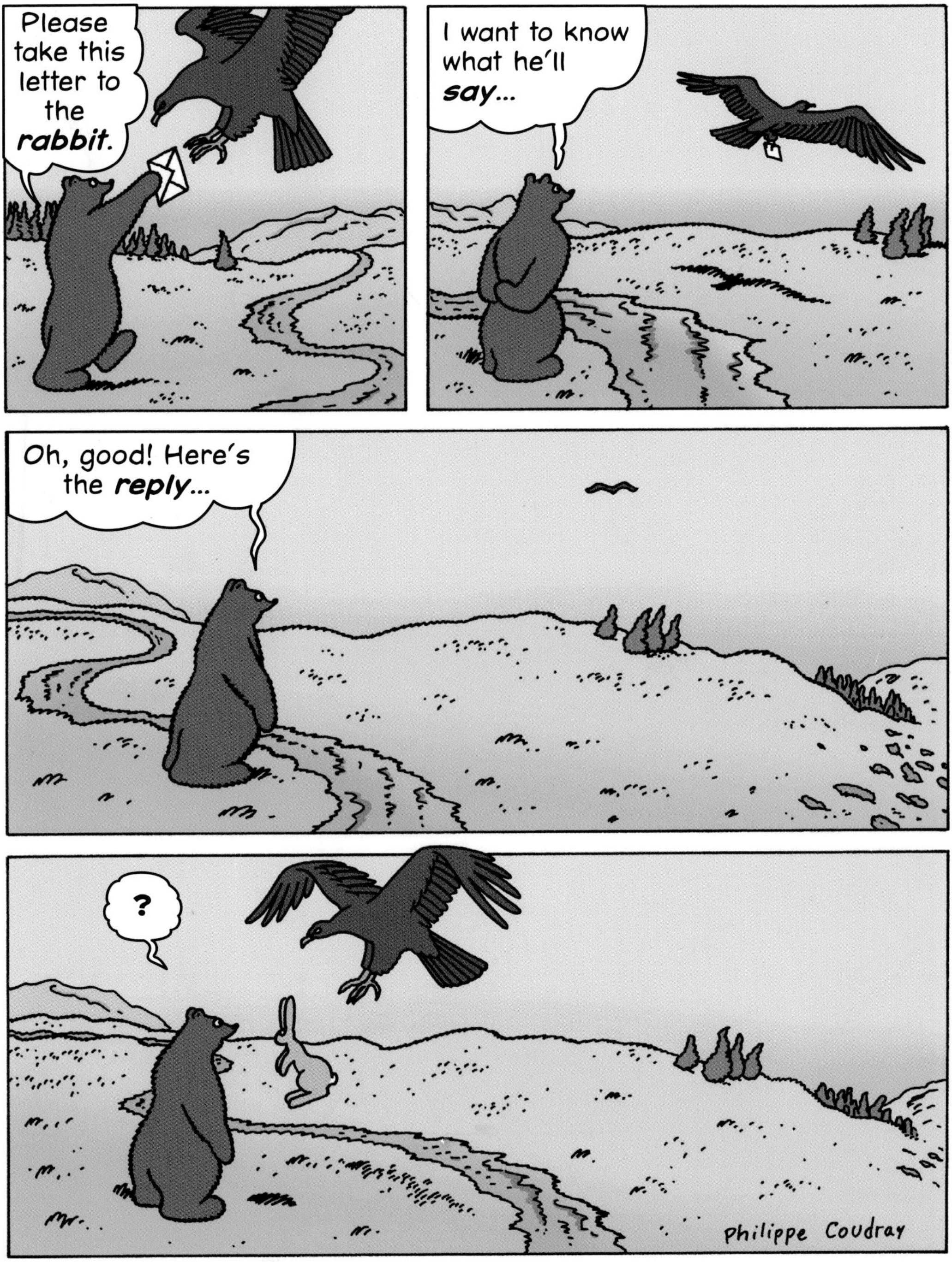
Please take this letter to the *rabbit*.
I want to know what he'll *say*...
Oh, good! Here's the *reply*...
?
Philippe Coudray

## *Ringleader*

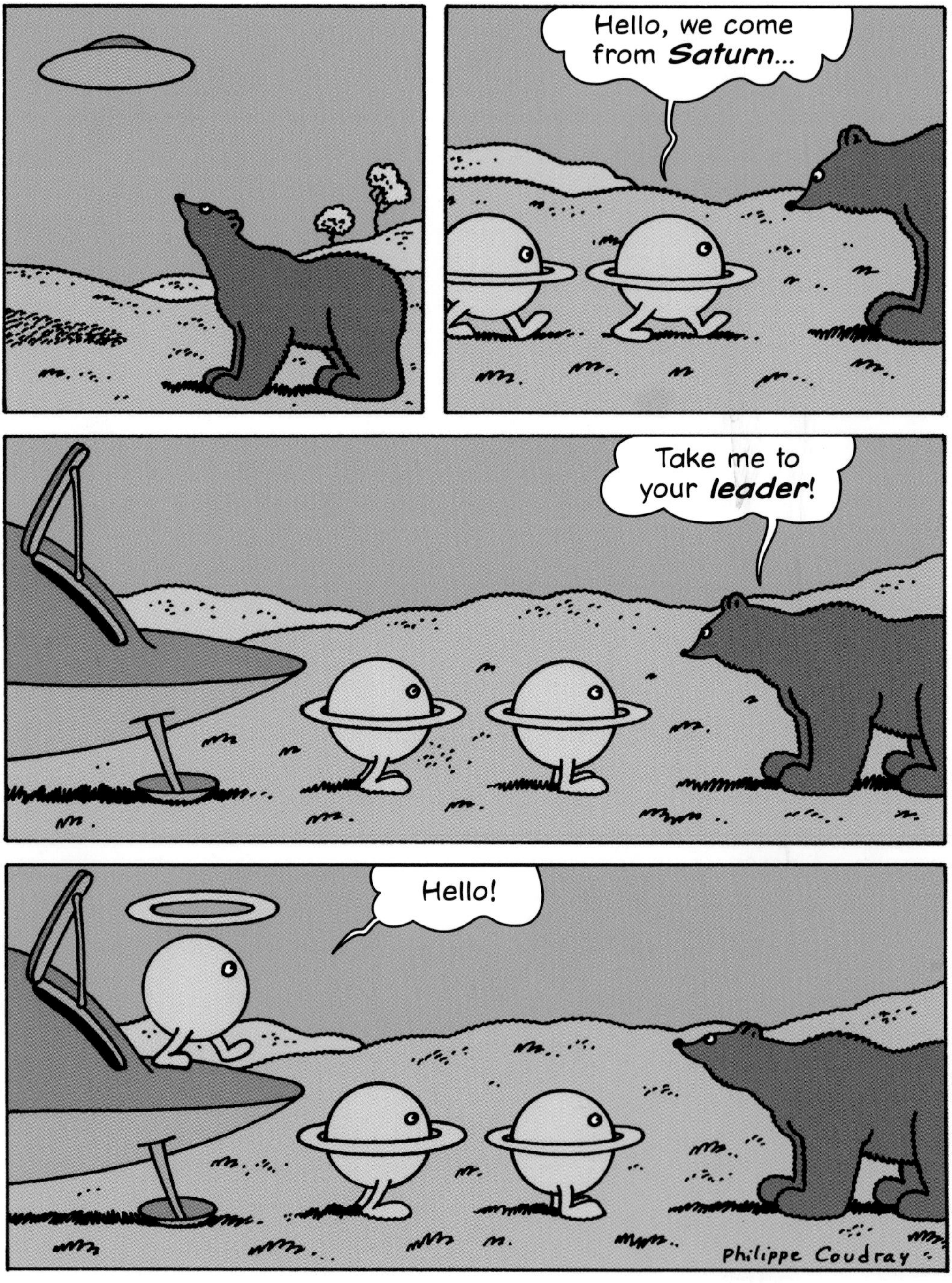
Hello, we come from *Saturn*...
Take me to your *leader*!
Hello!
Philippe Coudray

## *Reflection*

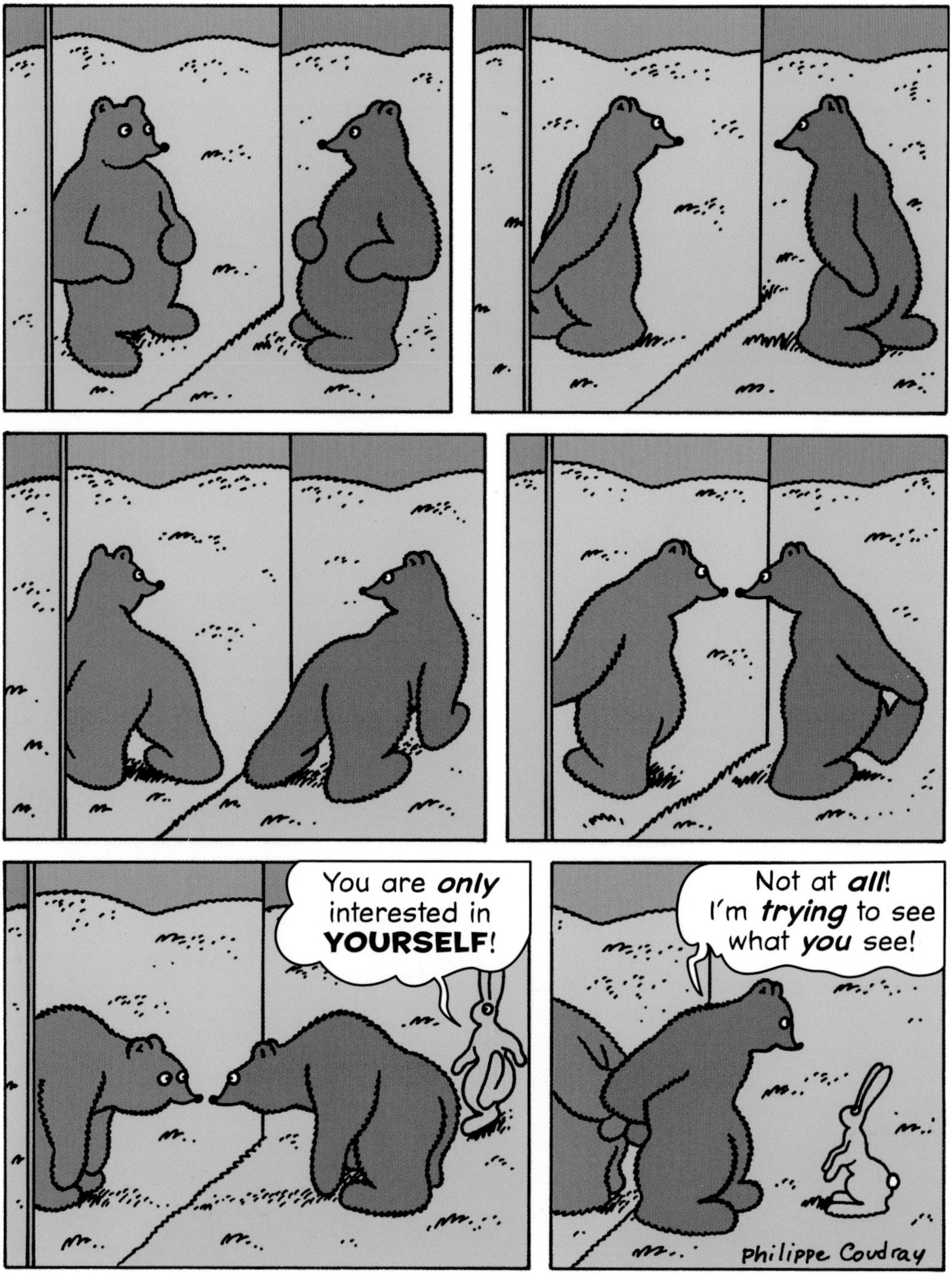
You are *only* interested in **YOURSELF**!
Not at ***all***! I'm ***trying*** to see what ***you*** see!
Philippe Coudray

## All tied up

Philippe Coudray

28

## A gift for you

Philippe Coudray

## *Bird-watching*

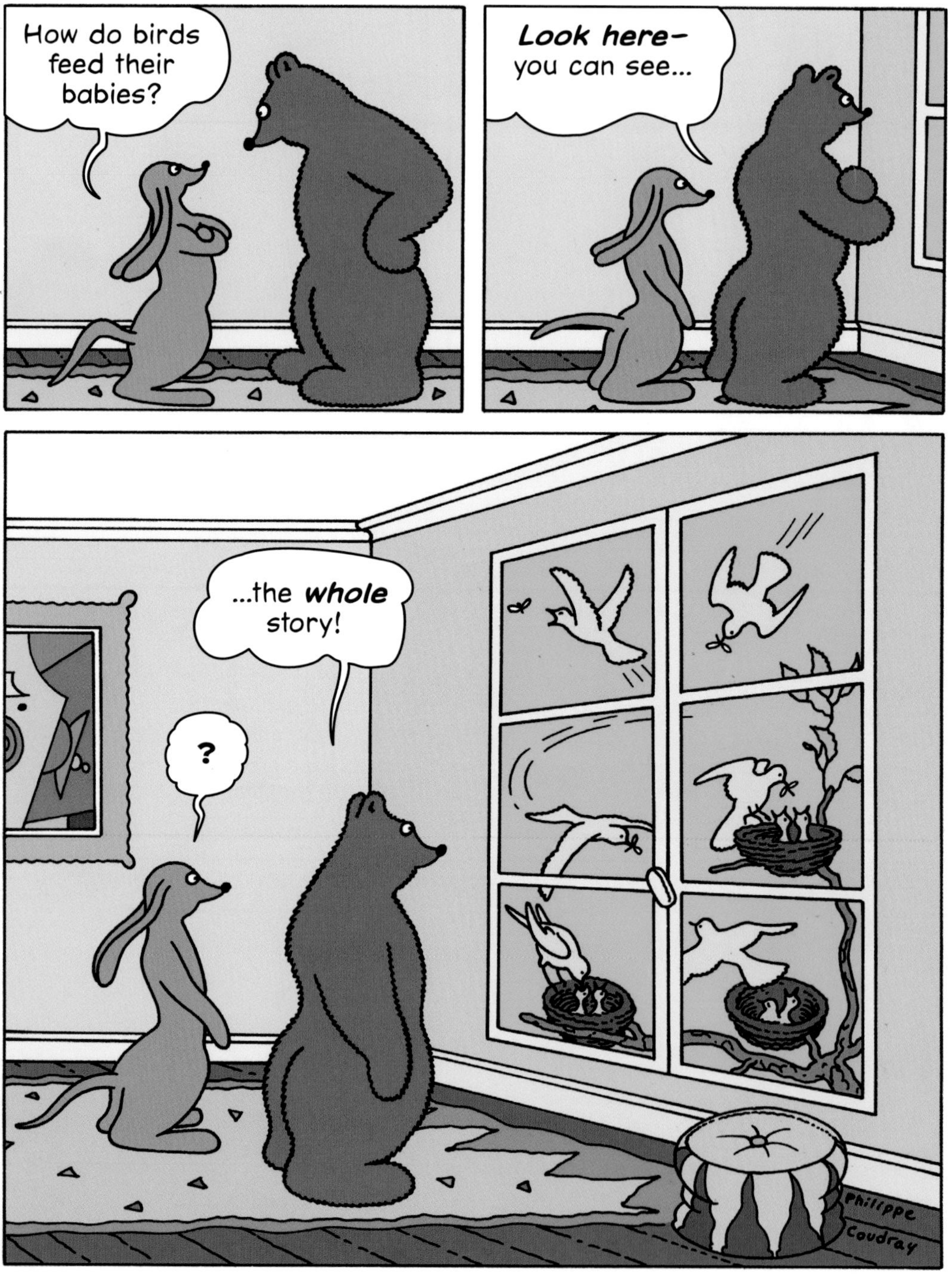
How do birds feed their babies?
*Look here–* you can see...
...the *whole* story!
?
Philippe Coudray

## Too smart for his own good

**THE END**

# ABOUT THE AUTHOR

**PHILIPPE COUDRAY** loves drawing comics and working with his twin brother Jean-Luc, who is also a humorist. Philippe's books are often used in the schools of France, his home country, where Benjamin Bear's French cousin, Barnabé, has won many prizes. In the U.S., *Benjamin Bear in Fuzzy Thinking* was nominated for an Eisner Award.

When he was younger, Philippe spent many of his family vacations in the mountains. He says, "I wanted to write a story about a bear because I love drawing the mountains where they live." In addition to his annual trip to Canada in search of Bigfoot, he enjoys creating stereoscopic images, and researching mythical creatures and other strange beasts.

# TIPS FOR PARENTS AND TEACHERS:
# HOW TO READ COMICS WITH KIDS

Kids **love** comics! They are naturally drawn to the details in the pictures, which make them want to read the words. Comics beg for repeated readings and let both emerging and reluctant readers enjoy complex stories with a rich vocabulary. But since comics have their own grammar, here are a few tips for reading them with kids:

GUIDE YOUNG READERS: Use your finger to show your place in the text, but keep it at the bottom of the speaking character so it doesn't hide the very important facial expressions.

HAM IT UP! Think of the comic book story as a play and don't hesitate to read with expression and intonation. Assign parts or get kids to supply the sound effects, a great way to reinforce phonics skills.

LET THEM GUESS. Comics provide lots of context for the words, so emerging readers can make informed guesses. Like jigsaw puzzles, comics ask readers to make connections, so check a young audience's understanding by asking, "What's this character thinking?" (but don't be surprised if a kid finds some of the comics' subtle details faster than you).

TALK ABOUT THE PICTURES. Point out how the artist paces the story with pauses (silent panels) or speeded-up action (a burst of short panels). Discuss how the size and shape of the panels carry meaning.

ABOVE ALL, ENJOY! There is of course never one right way to read, so go for the shared pleasure. Once children make the story happen in their imagination, they have discovered the thrill of reading, and you won't be able to stop them. At that point, just go get them more books, and more comics.

## www.TOON-BOOKS.com

SEE OUR FREE ONLINE CARTOON MAKERS,
LESSON PLANS, AND MUCH MORE.

# TOON INTO READING!™

## LEVEL 1

GRADES K–1

LEXILE BR–100 • GUIDED READING E–J • READING RECOVERY 7–12

### FIRST COMICS FOR BRAND-NEW READERS

- 200–300 easy sight words
- short sentences
- often one character
- single time frame or theme
- 1–2 panels per page

## LEVEL 2

GRADES 1–2

LEXILE BR–240 • GUIDED READING G–K • READING RECOVERY 11–18

### EASY-TO-READ COMICS FOR EMERGING READERS

- 300–700 words
- short sentences and repetition
- story arc with few characters in a small world
- 1–4 panels per page

## LEVEL 3

GRADES 2–3

LEXILE 150–300 • GUIDED READING K–P • READING RECOVERY 18–20

### CHAPTER-BOOK COMICS FOR ADVANCED BEGINNERS

- 800–1000+ words in long sentences
- long story divided in chapters
- broad world as well as shifts in time and place
- reader needs to make connections and speculate

# COLLECT THEM ALL!

## LEVEL 1  FIRST COMICS FOR BRAND-NEW READERS

## LEVEL 2  EASY-TO-READ COMICS FOR EMERGING READERS

   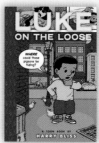 

## LEVEL 3  CHAPTER-BOOK COMICS FOR ADVANCED BEGINNERS

## TOON BOOKS

| | |
|---|---|
| **Set 1 • 10 hardcover books** | **978-1-61479-147-8** |
| Benny and Penny in Just Pretend | 978-1-61479-148-5 |
| Benny and Penny in the Toy Breaker | 978-1-61479-149-2 |
| Chick & Chickie Play All Day! | 978-1-61479-150-8 |
| Jack and the Box | 978-1-61479-151-5 |
| Mo and Jo Fighting Together Forever | 978-1-61479-152-2 |
| | |
| **Set 2 • 8 hardcover books** | **978-1-61479-298-7** |
| Benjamin Bear in Fuzzy Thinking | 978-1-61479-299-4 |
| Benny and Penny in the Big No-No! | 978-1-61479-300-7 |
| Little Mouse Gets Ready | 978-1-61479-301-4 |
| Luke on the Loose | 978-1-61479-302-1 |
| | |
| **Set 3 • 6 hardcover books** | **978-1-61479-422-6** |
| Benjamin Bear in Bright Ideas! | 978-1-61479-423-3 |
| Benny and Penny in Lights Out! | 978-1-61479-424-0 |
| The Big Wet Balloon | 978-1-61479-425-7 |

| | |
|---|---|
| Nina in That Makes Me Mad! | 978-1-61479-153-9 |
| Otto's Orange Day | 978-1-61479-154-6 |
| Silly Lilly and the Four Seasons | 978-1-61479-155-3 |
| Silly Lilly in What Will I Be Today? | 978-1-61479-156-0 |
| Zig and Wikki in Something Ate My Homework | 978-1-61479-157-7 |
| Maya Makes a Mess | 978-1-61479-303-8 |
| Patrick in a Teddy Bear's Picnic and Other Stories | 978-1-61479-304-5 |
| The Shark King | 978-1-61479-305-2 |
| Zig and Wikki in the Cow | 978-1-61479-306-9 |
| Otto's Backwards Day | 978-1-61479-426-4 |
| Patrick Eats His Peas and Other Stories | 978-1-61479-427-1 |
| A Trip to the Bottom of the World with Mouse | 978-1-61479-428-8 |